If There's Anyone Left

Volume 2

IF THERE'S ANYONE LEFT: VOLUME 2

Science and Speculative Fiction Short Story Magazine
Edited by Jason P. Burnham and C.M. Fields
https://www.iftheresanyoneleft.com

Want to make sure there is a Volume 3? Donate!
https://www.iftheresanyoneleft.com/donate

CONTENTS

EDITORIAL

Welcome to the second (!) volume of If There's Anyone Left. Volume 1 was incredible and we're so happy to be doing this again! We are once again honored to have such excellent authors send us their fantastic work. We look forward to making a third volume.

Our goal is to support people of color, the LGBTQ+ community, members of marginalized genders, and disabled people, to bring their voices for others to hear because we love them and they are powerful. We're so glad to share these stories with you. All proceeds from this volume will go toward funding Volume 3, so please share with your friends, family, and the world!

-The Editors

Nine Lives

by P.A. Cornell

One:

The first time we meet, I'm seven. Mom and I are heading back from dinner. I hear a faint mew, and mom checks the trashcan in the alley. We see you for the first time, all black with three white spots on your head.

"He won't live long," Mom says. "But we can care for him until then."

We make you a shoebox bed, padded by that ugly sweater I got from Aunt Lila, and keep you company until the end. Afterwards Mom puts the lid on the box, and we head to the backyard.

But we find you in the kitchen, a black kitten with three white spots on his head. You meow with energy this time. Mom opens the box to find just the sweater. I bury it anyway. I always hated that thing.

Two:

You follow me everywhere. I'm nine when I find the old well. I remove the rotted boards and look down at filthy water. Then I climb on top and run around the edge. But when I try to stop, I can't. The world keeps moving and I feel myself falling. I expect to hit water but instead I feel a push, and I'm on the ground.

I look down into the well in time to see you sinking beneath the water.

I call your name.

After a moment there's a meow. I turn to see you sitting behind me, a kitten again.

Three:

In your third life you grow to a respectable sixteen. I'm back from college and notice you sleep more than you used to. Mom says you aren't eating much. The vet diagnoses kidney disease—says you're in pain.

I can't let you suffer, but I stay with you, just like that first time. You pass on in my arms, purring all the while.

"Hey there," I say, when I find you sitting in my car, a kitten once more. I scratch you between the ears like you like, right over those white spots.

Four:

My girlfriend Alice moves into our apartment. She's never had a cat, but you win her over. We become a family.

One day I come home to find Alice crying. She tells me through sobs that without thinking she left the balcony door open. You fell from the tenth floor.

Before I can console her, I hear a high-pitched *mew* from the bedroom. I take her in there and show her you're fine.

"There's something you should know," I say.

Five:

I thought you'd be jealous of Mark when Alice and I brought him home, but you're not. You don't even mind when he pulls your tail. At night you sleep by his crib, guarding your new brother.

It's this protectiveness that causes the end of your fifth life. Mark's in his stroller while Alice checks the mail. You're walking next to them, as is your habit. Then the stroller rolls away toward the street. Alice runs but you're faster. You jump and let the car hit you instead, causing the driver to stop.

Alice picks you up and wraps you in a baby blanket. When she walks in the door, there you are. She shakes out the blanket and finds it empty.

Six:
Two years later, you're outside when a snowstorm hits. You're gone for three days. When you return, you're sick. We take you to your latest vet who diagnoses pneumonia. He doesn't expect you to survive, and you don't.
This time I find you in Mark's lap.
"Baby kitty, Daddy!"
"Yes. He does that sometimes," I say.

Seven:
You've always been a risk-taker. You go places you shouldn't. During life seven, you venture into the woods to prove you can take on a coyote. You can't. You're in rough shape when I find you. Gone before I get you home. But inside, there you are, curled up by the fireplace returned to youth.
"Be more careful next time," I say.

Eight:
I'm not sure what ends your eighth life. I just come home one day, after dropping Mark off at a party, to find you young again.

Nine:
We're both old now. Alice has been gone a while, and Mark is busy with his husband and kids, so we don't see him often. But we're good company, you and I. We live a relaxed life, curled up on the couch, you purring and me snoring. Sometimes I wonder which one of us will go first. You've already beat your record. They say cats have nine lives, so I wonder if this is it for you. Still, I think you've had a good run. So have I, for that matter.
I scratch your head between your ears, right above those three white spots, like you like. You lick my hand and purr.

About the Author

P.A. Cornell is a Chilean-Canadian SFF writer and personal assistant to her cats, Jax and Rebel, who got their names from two of her characters. A member of the SFWA and graduate of the Odyssey writing workshop, her short fiction has appeared in several anthologies and genre magazines. For a full bibliography visit pacornell.com.

Heronry

by Clio Velentza

My father was the last of the grey heron men. He was, as such, deathless on his own, but those days did not set store by gods.

Only once in my life I ever saw him in his man form— that day my ship had docked in Egypt. I remember seeing the grey herons land in the swamp like smoke, mercury-soft and thin, their beaks slicing the air like blades. One by one they alighted on the shore and changed into men as the sun set. I thought – so many, so many, my father's brothers, my own enchanted kin – how their darting bodies gleamed! I was so young, I could not know they were the last.

I was born in a deadly time for miracles, though the human women still adored the heron men, and begged them for their children. And if the women did not protest that the boys were born in eggs, and shed their bird form only in the strange lands they wintered in, it was because we heron-daughters were said to be of famous and enviable grace.

Quietly, I had watched them through the spyglass: I saw my father, grey and dark, laugh at the warm mud below him which swarmed with many scurrying treats. I wondered why they were not content, croaking to one another through the reeds all summer, hunting for frog and fish. Why should they come here as soon as the first snow fell? Why in this unfriendly land, where the sons of men hunted them down from the moment they had shed their wings? I hadn't seen my mother young, I did not know — that was what someone told me once. The heron men knew which longing eyes waited for them in the warm dappled courtyards, searching the skies all year with wild and lusty hope.

I heard their harsh cries now in the falling twilight, and watched them march ashore in their light hearts. And then they were swallowed by the city night, and this was the last that any of us saw of them. Many knives were bared that winter in the harbor, and jealous hands are swift.

Back in the North, trading for salt fish, I heard that the watchful eyes saw no grey herons return that winter. The wetlands had been still and strange. None of them flew or waded back. Only an old bow hunter later remembered a single, solitary bird. It hobbled back into the pond: a quiet, broken thing. Too weak to hunt for food it stood without moving, waited for him to approach and stared at him with scorn.

Naturally, the old man said, he shot it down for game.

About the Author

Clio Velentza is a writer from Athens, Greece. Her flash fiction has appeared in several literary journals, and has been a winner of Best Microfiction, *Wigleaf's* Top 50 and The Best Small Fictions. Her debut novel, "The Piano Room", is out now by Fairlight Books. You can find her on twitter at @clio_v

Do This

by Ulises Amaya

A brief history of humanity circa 2022, as told through clickbait.

-This may sound crazy, but fitness guru says do this one thing to lose belly fat

-Wall Street Traders have figured out how to beat the market using one simple trick

-Social Media Influencers are making money by doing this one easy thing

-Hackers infiltrating heavily encrypted database do this one thing to bypass any operating system

-Hair loss is a myth according to this surgeon, truth will leave you horrified

-Scientists have finally mapped the human genome, now saying do this one thing every day for a longer life

-Man who predicted the pandemic now says he's doing this one easy thing to prepare for the next global event

-Doctor who decoded the human brain now says to do this one easy thing to increase IQ

-Linguists hate him because he can learn any language in

three days by doing this one easy thing

-Famed musician and podiatrist reveals his secret for learning any instrument fast – Do this one easy thing once easily

-Man who predicted the pandemic horrified by hair loss lie, extends life and increases IQ, vows not to rest until…

-Archeologist discovers ancient Egyptian text, reveals the truth about cats, says they do this one thing every other day

-Doomsday Prepper has figured out number one tool for survival post-apocalypse

-World governments can't prevent hackers from learning truth about human knowledge, all advancements in history due to this one simple trick

-Legendary martial artist reveals his secret to perfect form, you won't believe how easy it is

-Prepare to be shocked! Former president makes startling death-bed confession, reveals truth to his success – Does one thing every day

-Man who predicted pandemic joined by Hackers and Man who can learn any language in three days, now known as The New Chosen, kidnap Archeologist, find long lost diary of the last King of Mali, says do this one thing for empiric manifestation – Not what you think!

-Prophet of God summoned, reveals hidden truth, says do this one thing every day to see Ideal Forms

-Cats phase out of existence, last meow is a warning

-Hellfire rains on Earth, millions slaughtered for their hubris, The New Chosen ascend on the wheels of chaos, say all must do this one simple thing

-God speaks, says the Prophet is false, says one easy trick leads to salvation

-Yama rises, says too many people have learned the truth in your area, will not rest until darkness reigns for a thousand generations

-The New Chosen are soul bonded into caverns of the underworld, cursed to do this one thing for eternity

-Malevolent Spirits roam the Earth rounding up Fitness Gurus, Social Media Influencers, and Mythbuster Surgeon, broadcast their deaths in Gladiatorial Games, weapon of choice is a shocker!

-Wall Street Traders have figured out how to beat the market, self-immolate in the streets using this one household ingredient

-Famed musician and podiatrist transcends multiverse using one obvious method

-Humans band together with Legendary Martial artist and Doomsday Prepper to fight the forces of evil, save humanity with this one weird tip

-In shocking twist, the great underpinning energy of the Universe begins imminent collapse due to power imbalance, do this one easy thing to coalesce your atomic material

-Man who predicted the end of all light and time says you should have listened to him, says you could have saved your loved ones, says it's not too late, says to do this one thing

-The Big Bang resets, emits faint pulse, says it holds all life in its core, but decides not to do anything

©2022 Ulises Amaya

About the Author

Ulises Amaya is a writer, musician, and teacher living in Queens, New York. His work has appeared in Flash Fiction Magazine and Center Stage Magazine. Recently he had a misunderstanding with a Mandoline slicer and it got the better of a couple finger tips. However, they have healed up nicely. For more information, please visit his website at http://www.ulisesamaya.com

The Dream Eater

By P.H. Low

One afternoon, you climb the stairs to your bedroom, brush away the dust beneath your childhood bed. A pair of eyes blinks back, guileless as a plush toy.

Hey, says the monster.

The pill bottle digs into your palm. *You're still here.*

I am, it replies.

You sit down, hard, on the floor. There is a stone in your throat. *I was never afraid of you.*

I know.

You watch each other, wary. Outside the window, robins chitter and dance; pine trees caress blue sky. Your father planted those trees fifteen years ago, a month before your birth; now, they overshadow the house.

There were always worse things to fear, you say eventually. *You were never going to hurt me.*

I know.

Downstairs, a laugh track blares at your mother, who's asleep. The pill bottle rattles in your fist.

The thing is, nothing really *happened*, up at the school. There was the other girls' cold silence, the teachers' smirks. The flask of rum you stole from under Cora's cot and chugged in one sitting. But none of it adds up to the hours you lay alone in your room, swathed in a fog of your own making. None of it explains why, two hundred miles away and safe in the walls of the house you grew up in, you still want to crawl out of your skin.

The feeling isn't new, exactly. But it has never drowned you before.

Look, the dust says, *I won't tell you what to do, but—*

But what? It comes out sharper than you intend.

It considers you, then, all feathered lint and gravity. You wonder for the first time what its nights have been like, this past year. If it has ever been lonely.

The thing about dreams, it says, *is that they fade. And one can only ever discover this when one wakes the next morning.*

Oh.

Below you, another laugh track plays. You tip your head back against the wall and just sit, until your calves prickle from poor circulation, until the stone in your throat softens enough to swallow. You're taking a gap year, your parents tell their friends—to expand your horizons, brush up on math. Only to each other, in the kitchen at night, do they whisper: *to convalesce.*

You cannot understand, yourself, why this sounds like a punishment.

I was reared on your sharpest nightmares, says the dust, quietly. *I can take them again.*

Can you?

It doesn't blink. *Try me.*

Outside, birds preen; the sky is an arch of blue. You unscrew the plastic cap, tip out the first capsule.

You have a vested interest, you say.

Yes, the dust replies. *But so do you.*

The pill is cool in your palm, bright and hard as a future. You weigh it, eggshell-light; imagine, for a moment, the burn as it twists against your being.

Then you toss it under the bed.

A dark mouth gapes to meet it, twelve glistening rows of teeth, and swallows it whole.

About the Author

P.H. Low is a Malaysian Chinese American writer with work published in *Strange Horizons, Tor.com, Fantasy Magazine,* and *If There's Anyone Left* Vol. 1, among others. P.H. attended Viable Paradise in 2019, and currently serves as a first reader for *khōréō*, a speculative fiction magazine featuring immigrant and diaspora writers and stories.

Animal Husbandry

By J.L. Akagi

At the kitchen table, Eliza Tashiro rhinestones her cheer skirt with toothpicks and a large brown bottle of Aleene's Fabric Fusion Permanent Adhesive. Every Halloween costume and cheerleading outfit that Eliza has ever worn has come from this bottle.

Eliza dips the very tip of the toothpick into the glue that gathers near the rim, then paints a thin coat over the flat back of a rhinestone before pressing it to the hem of her skirt. Each rhinestone gets a new toothpick, and Eliza has a neat stack of gluey toothpicks laid out over a tissue.

When Eliza was a girl, she used to lie in bed idly cleaning her gums with toothpicks. She stuck her discarded toothpicks into the side of the mattress. So many built up that her room became infested with two-inch samurai that used the toothpicks as swords to stab Eliza until she picked up her mess.

Eliza must have learned her lesson. Most of the girls on the cheer squad use hot glue; it's easier. But messy. Their rhinestones are ringed with clear thermoplastic. Meanwhile, Eliza fastidiously swabs excess glue with a q-tip soaked in nail polish.

"The acetone is going to bleach the fabric," her mom says from across the table. She is responsible for Eliza's top, spurring the block letters with domed rhinestones so big and round they look like engagement diamonds.

At least, that's what the cheer captain had said when she picked them for the "spring spruce up" of their uniforms. *Don't they remind you of engagement rings, girls?* Everyone speculates that Matt Chung, Eliza's boyfriend, will ask Eliza to marry him after graduation. Like it's an all-Asian episode of *Leave It to Beaver* or something.

Eliza dreads it.

Eliza considers the end of her cotton swabs, flushed pink from the red polyester. "If it bleaches the fabric, then it'll make the rhinestones look bigger."

"Yes, call attention to your hips. Let Matt know they're ready to make babies."

"The hips aren't really the part of my anatomy that can make babies. And what do you know about boys? You're not—" Eliza stops herself before she says something nasty. "You ordered Dad in a catalogue."

"No catalogue," her mom scoffs. "I answered a help wanted ad. I remember each word. Help wanted: one irritable schoolteacher who can't cook and hates housekeeping to—"

"—to nag your future daughter about how that daughter performs femininity while failing at it herself. Inquire within."

Eliza's mom smooths the front of her cardigan, creased from sitting. "If I'm failing at 'performing femininity,' then at least I have an audience."

"Not that kind of performance, Mom. It's a constant and stylized recursive pattern of acts that mimic dominant gender conventions."

"Where are you learning all this crap?"

"Zines." Eliza grins. "And your bitching."

"It's not bitching, it's preparing you to live under someone's thumb. Could be Matt's thumb, if you're not careful."

Eliza winces. It's not that she doesn't like Matt—she does. Matt Chung is captain of the basketball team, and the best-looking player at that. The kind of Asian guy who is allowed to be considered attractive because he defies Asian stereotypes. Tall, broad, with perfect teeth and a boisterous personality. She likes it when everyone compliments what a nice, matching pair they make.

But she can't really talk to him about the things that bother her. Like rhinestone glue and toothpick samurai.

Eliza changes the subject. "I'd been meaning to ask you, did you hear about the crane wife?"

"No. Does it have Julia Roberts in it?"

"It's not a movie, Mom. It's a...well, I guess it's a tabloid story. About a crane in Japan. Have you heard about it?"

"I used to be a crane, you know."

"Yeah, duh. That's why I brought it up." Eliza isn't annoyed. This is just how they talk to each other. "This man in—I think it's Osaka—he finds this injured crane and nurses it back to health. It gets better and he releases it. Then, like, the next day—"

"Was it the next day or was it *like* the next day?"

Eliza narrows her eyes at her mom. "*Approximately* the next day, a woman shows up at his door wanting to marry him. And they get married and this wife weaves beautiful silk kimono. They sell really well so the husband asks for more and more. She's basically up every night weaving while he sleeps."

"I'm out of rhinestones. Give me some."

Eliza slides the plastic bin of rhinestones towards her mom. "Anyway, she gets sick, and he doesn't even notice until she starts making less kimono—"

"Fewer," her mom corrects.

"*So*, one night he sneaks into her room to see what's slowing her down and finds a crane at the loom, picking feathers off her body to weave into the kimono."

Only now does Eliza realize she's accidentally glued a rhinestone to her thumbnail. It nestles in the white curve of her nailbed, the lunula. She tries to scrape it off, but the nail cracks and feather spurts up from the split. White, but dewy with blood. Eliza plucks it out and discards it with the toothpicks.

When she looks up, her mom is scowling, cateye glasses casting shadows over her full-moon cheeks. Her mom catches Eliza's stare and waves it away in a distinctly Japanese gesture. "I read a story like that, in *Shūkan Gendai,* but it's about a clam."

"Okay, how does that one go?"

"A beautiful woman mysteriously appears on a man's doorstep, begging to be his wife. He agrees, and the woman makes him a delicious clam stew every night."

"Okay…"

"One day he sneaks up on her in the kitchen to see how it's prepared and catches her pissing clam juice into the pot."

Eliza throws a handful of dry toothpicks at her mom. "Oh, Mom. Gross. You just made that up."

"Did not. Cranes and clams become wives all the time."

"It's still gross."

About the Author

J.L. Akagi is a queer Japanese American who writes about what scares her. She lives with her wife and two chihuahuas in New York. Her work has appeared in *Strange Horizons* and *DreamForge Anvil.* She can be contacted at jlinakagi@gmail.com

In the Garden of Rings

by Tara Campbell

Momma's always told me not to try planting a ring on my own. I've watched her thrust her hands into the dirt for years now, loosening the soil, shaping a hole, then rummaging through her little box of rings for one to bury. Even now, she only lets me watch, never telling me exactly what she's wishing for with each ring. Even though I'm grown enough to help with all the other chores around the house. Even after I became a woman myself in that messy, red way about which she simply said, "Well, here we go" before handing me a pad.

Momma's tight-lipped about most things, but especially the rings. It's like she's jealous of anyone else having her power; and I suppose she is, since she went to the trouble to grow a dragon to watch over our farm. All Momma's ever shared is that she can only have three ring wishes at a time, and she's not trading in the house or the dragon, so she only has the one ring crop a year to play with, one free wish at a time, and that's why I'm not to touch her box of rings.

Each spring she plants a ring and we watch it grow, me eager to find out what the wish is, her anxious to see what it will actually look like. One year a whole field of corn sprouted from a yellow solitaire diamond ring, each ear studded with pearls instead of kernels, except for the one that held another ring. Momma put that ring in her box and sold most of the pearls. We made enough to feed ourselves and the dragon, and still add to our nest egg in the bank. Momma kept the ones she didn't sell in an inflatable pool in the basement for the dragon to watch over, and sometimes when she was in a good mood we'd step in and splash around in our own little sea of pearls. Not anymore, though, now that I'm grown. She says she's keeping them for my future. Funny, though: the dragon never lets me take any of them out of the house.

Another year, a ruby ring resulted in a single pomegranate tree. Our dragon wrapped itself around that tree, and we spent the summer picking the plump red fruits, splitting their skins open and scooping dozens of diamonds out of sticky magenta pulp. Still, Momma didn't really relax until we opened the fruit that held another ring. No matter that the ring box was never empty; Momma couldn't truly enjoy the harvest until it produced one more seed for the future. She insisted on finding it, even the year she grew the dragon.

I was still small then, eight or nine, but I will never forget her planting the emerald ring, then watching in amazement week after week as the tips of the beast's horns sprouted, then earth fell away from the scaly skin of its forehead, then the day it finally opened its eyes and trained those glistening red orbs on me. Momma'd rush out to the fields every time it breathed fire, searching the previous year's scorched stalks for a flash of metal or a glittering stone. Turns out we just had to be patient, then hold our noses and sift. I hate to think how many dungpiles we soiled ourselves with—me, at my age, barely as tall as the piles—before the ring finally emerged.

After that, I thought she'd finally be a little less tense, less guarded with a dragon to do the guarding for us. I couldn't have put it into words then, but I guess I hoped I'd finally get a mother who could focus on me for a change, rather than watching out for the neighbors or fingering through that ring box mulling over what to wish for next. I know she was just looking out for me, in her own way, but I always felt kind of like an afterthought. Even then I had the sense I wasn't something she'd specifically wished for. I'd never been one of her rings.

But now I'm grown, in that red, messy way we never discussed; and there's someone else out there, someone Momma doesn't know about, who makes me feel like I was wished right down from the stars. I've been going out to meet this someone past the edge of the farm, beyond anyplace our dragon cares about, and I've been telling this girl every wish I have, about exploring the big wide world, and finding a home, a real home with love and hugs and kisses, arms around one another, eyes closed for a moment of comfort and peace.

I asked Momma last night what she was going to plant this spring. She told me not to worry my little head about it, that she and the dragon would decide. Her eyes gleamed red in the hearth fire as she explained how I'd understand one day, when this farm was mine and I had a young woman of my own to protect. Her bony fingers gripped the ring box like claws.

So now I'm off to plant my own ring. Not one from Momma's box—the dragon almost snapped off my hand when I tried to take one in the wee hours of the morning. Same for the pearls that were supposedly for my future. Funny, though, the dragon didn't seem to care at all when I left with a bag slung over my shoulder holding my two favorite dresses, a change of shoes, and a bit of food to last until whatever happens next.

I won't forget Momma's advice: I won't plant a ring on my own. I will wear my love's ring, and she'll wear mine; and we'll find our own plot of land, dig our hands into the dirt, and grow our own future, together.

About the Author

Tara Campbell is a writer, teacher, Kimbilio Fellow, and fiction co-editor at *Barrelhouse*. She received her MFA from American University. Previous publication credits include *SmokeLong Quarterly*, *Masters Review*, *Wigleaf*, *Jellyfish Review*, *Booth*, *Strange Horizons*, and *If There's Anyone Left* Vol 1. She's the author of a novel, *TreeVolution*, and four collections: *Circe's Bicycle*, *Midnight at the Organporium*, *Political AF: A Rage Collection*, and *Cabinet of Wrath: A Doll Collection*. Connect with her at www.taracampbell.com or on Twitter: @TaraCampbellCom

A Beginner's Guide to Jailbreaking Your myToast3000™

By Aimee Ogden

With the labor stoppages at licensed myToast proprietary production facilities, a lot of people out there have found themselves bereft at breakfast. Maybe you're reading this to stick it to Kitchen Creative Services, Inc. on behalf of the workers who are on strike; maybe you're reading this because you're hungry; I don't really care. Either way, here are your options for making your $700 paperweight into a functioning custom toast-art producer again.

METHOD A

(Heads up: off-label use is going to void your warranty.)

1. **Buy some pre-sliced bread.** It's the best thing since itself. Or go wild and make your own, but realistically you're not on wikiHow trying to jailbreak your smart toaster because you're a kitchen whiz, are you?

2. **Carefully remove the aluminum wrapper from a slice of a myToast proprietary loaf.** Don't tear the paper or you'll have to start over (with this step, not the buying pre-sliced bread one). I suggest steaming the sticky seam open. Just be careful not to let the wrapper get too wet or you're going to be cleaning a bread slurry off of it before you can move on to Step 3.

3. **Adjust the store-bought bread to the size of**

the myToast slice. You can try a (clean) nail file. Be gentle, and DON'T FORGET to check depth as well as height and width! If your bread is too thicc you might start a fire; please do not sue me, I'm just a poor unemployed college student, and I like having money to eat and pay bus fare, thanks.

4. **Clean up the bread dust.** Again: don't start a fire, don't sue me, don't take my grocery money.

5. **Wrap your store-bought bread in the proprietary wrapper.** Make sure the myToast logo is centered on the bread: that's where the RFID chip is located. I still haven't figured out a way to get the RFID out of the wrapper without damaging it. Nor a way to stick an RFID to a naked piece of bread for the duration of a toasting.

6. **Carefully lower the re-wrapped slice into the myToast slot.** You'll feel a slight give in the support bar when the RFID has successfully scanned. Make sure the edges of the wrapper don't get caught in the heating element. Fire bad, etc. etc. etc.

7. **Choose your toast settings.** Select your preferred toast done-ness and the toasting pattern. (I hope you're not going to set it to 'light' after all this work.)

8. **Voila!** You made toast with the Death Star or whatever on it. Yay. Apply it to your face.

METHOD B

1. **Connect your myToast to your smartphone and download the UrToast app.** It's only $1.99 USD because even people who know how to crack smart toasters have to eat and this is a Doofus Tax for dropping $700 on a toaster that's going to hold your grilled cheese hostage. (Yes, before you ask, unlicensed software installs will

also void your warranty.)

2. **Shhh, don't whine.** Let's be real: wouldn't you rather give me two dollars than spend the markup on myToast proprietary loaves for the rest of your life, and/or your toaster's life (but realistically that thing is going to outlive us both, it's basically the Terminator with a bagel setting)? Bonus: comes with a security packet to beef up the native antivirus install so that you never have to delay breakfast until you've paid off a Russian ransomware demand. I have a lot of time on my hands these days and it turns out I'm kind of good at this stuff, so hey, we both benefit.

3. **Don't forget to rate in the app store afterward.** You're a peach. Enjoy that toast; you've earned it.

About the Author

Aimee Ogden is a former science teacher and software tester; now she writes stories about sad astronauts and angry princesses. Her novellas "Sun-Daughters, Sea-Daughters" and "Local Star" debuted in 2022 from Tor.com and Interstellar Flight Press respectively, and her short fiction has also appeared in magazines such as *Clarkesworld*, *Analog*, and *Beneath Ceaseless Skies*. With Bennett North, she co-edits *Translunar Travelers Lounge*, a magazine of fun and optimistic speculative fiction.

Sonoran

by E.G. Condé

Personal Log. EID#0918201-29910. Surname: Tso. Given Name: Eden.

Mother once said I ought to "live my truth". And so that is what I'm going to do. There's no turning back now. Maybe someone, someday will want to know what drove me beyond the Verge. And so, I share my story, so that you, whoever you are, may understand what it is to live in fear of the light of your sun.

It began 33 years ago with my birth, yes, a live birth, out there in the pastel veldts, when green was more than a memory. Sometimes I remember the shadows of vaulting hawks cascading over rosy buttes, I remember the sun, when it was not yet too bright to see. I remember Mother and the stories she told about her basket-weaving foremothers in the centuries before. Like so many others, the Bright made my home unlivable. So, Mother sent me on the caravans bound for the Megalopolis of the Sun, where the CEO of Astral promised safe refuge for all willing to work.

My youthful eyes were not prepared for the great wonders of the City; towering palms, crystalline fountains, and grass, emerald blades jutting up from lawns beneath a dome of engineered glass called the Verge. Astral engineers explained that the Verge absorbed much of the excess heat and ultraviolet radiation emitted by our star in the aftermath of that disastrous attempt by scientists to repair our warming climate.

For a time, I was happy. The city air was clean and

cool. Water flowed everywhere, endlessly recycled to prevent scarcity. Astral hired me as a construction monitor for the outermost fringes of the City, where the Verge, too, was expanding, like a bubble about to burst into the wrecked wastes beyond. I spent my days on lofty scaffoldings, watching the metallic exoskeletons of drones as they sculpted the land, as they dropped modular structures into sockets, as they printed supporting beams and roofs from the molten metals spooling in their cnidarian bodies. I monitored their progress on my ocular display, adjusting their outputs when necessary to compensate for resource shortages. I spent most of my time entranced by the industry of these machines that floated about like xeric jellyfish, laboring to expand the megalopolis.

Ximene was the first monitor to notice that the Bright was accelerating. They told me once, over tea and arepas, that Astral was exploring new measures to compensate.

"Environmental control is as good as it is going to get," They said to me, viridian eyes watering, "so they're looking into...augmentation."

"What kind of augmentation?" I asked.

Ximene pointed to a bobbing drone glinting over a rooftop. "Those drones are perfectly insulated against these conditions. But we, we're just...flesh."

"And Astral wants to change that?" I said, admiring the paleness of their skin.

"Exactly," Ximene nodded. "They'll start with artificial pigmentation then transition to metabolic implants."

"Doesn't sound so bad," I said, gesturing to the drone in the midst of lifting a structure into place, "as long as we don't end up like them."

"Yeah," Ximene chuckled.

Over the next year, the Bright intensified exponentially. Ximene was the first to undergo augmentation. Their skin had become darker than mine was at birth. We met for drinks. Later that night, I felt my pain soothed by their delicate touch. My scorched skin was not yet too burned to feel.

Nestled in the crook of my arm, Ximene whispered to me their fears and hopes and dreams.

Do you ever wonder what it's like out there?"

"I remember it," I say, reminding them that I am not a native urbanite.

"I'm sorry about your mother," Ximene said, hugging their knees.

"You're deflecting. Tell me what you're thinking."

"I found a way to go out there," Ximene said, handing me a schematic.

I shook my head in revulsion. "It's unnatural."

"What is natural anymore?"

When Ximene didn't report to their shift the next day, I knew what they had done. I went to the engineering lab, finding their lifeless body splayed amid a mess of wires jutting out from tiny perforations in their skull. I did not cry or scream, instead, I called up the real-time drone tracker on my ocular. One unit's trajectory diverged significantly from the others. I left the lab at a sprint, making my way to the edge of the construction zone, where a single drone buoyed unsteadily toward the barrier.

"Ximene!" I shouted.

The sinuous drone drifted, unresponsive to my pleas. In an instant it had bored its way through the membrane of glass, its chrome bulk deliquescing into the cross-blur of the heat mirages beyond.

EDEN. My comm unit thrummed. IT'S MORE BEAUTIFUL THAN I IMAGINED. It was Ximene's garbled voice. I WISH YOU WERE HERE WITH ME. THE WIND SOUNDS – The transmission abruptly cascaded into static. I heard the sky quake, then came the smoke, boring through the fissured glass in wiry tendrils. Ximene was gone.

After Ximene's death, Astral announced that behavioral implants to prevent "thermally-induced psychosis" would soon become mandatory. Astral confiscated Ximene's schematic as part of their investigation into what had transpired. It wasn't long before other monitors like Ximene started disappearing. I knew what was happening but I refused to believe it. Astrals. That's what they were calling themselves now. The corporation was offering an "ascension" bonus to employees willing to augment themselves.

At night, I dream of being forced to become one of those tentacular abominations. I dream of Ximene's lifeless body. I dream of my mother and dimmer skies and puffy clouds and pronged saguaros and the beauty of the world that was. And now, I finally understand what I must do to be free. So, I journey out into the Sonoran, beyond the ersatz bounds of the megalopolis to surrender to the scorching bright of our star, so that I can be reborn like a phoenix in the fires of creation, where Ximene and my foremothers await me in a world of unbridled light.

About the Author

E.G. Condé (he/him) is an Anthropologist of technology and a queer boricua imagineer of speculative fiction, fantasy, and horror. His short fiction appears in *Anthropology & Humanism* and *Reckoning*. When he isn't conjuring up faraway universes or nearly possible futures, you might find him traversing the world in search of sand dunes to hike on.

Travel Guide to Spaceport Rest Stops

By Seoung Kim

The Sunken Spire

I HATE stopping here. Every time I try to hold it and fly right by, and every time the pressure in my bladder becomes unbearable when the ziggurat rises into view. It's probably part of the curse that the last empress left on the place as she was dragged screaming from her throne by the Undying Priesthood.

Anyway, the lights are never working. 1/10.

#

Proxima B

No one stays in Proxima B long. The bathrooms are the main feature: two full floors of them in addition to a food court. Lots of chirpy ads on the backs of stalls. Their security system is also robust, what with all the pirates and smugglers who pass through.

Have to say, I've never encountered such well-made sinks. Didn't even shatter when port authority bodyslammed me into one. I want a word with whoever's in charge of cleaning, though-- nearly slipped and fell on a wet floor while I was running. It's common courtesy to leave a sign up, you know? 7/10.

#

Huo Niao Cluster

Achingly gorgeous. Stands by itself in the middle of a

golden field. I had been awake all night flying and I thought it must be a dream.

My home planet is a bit of a trash fire, so I don't know what I was getting all nostalgic about. Really wish I could have stayed longer, but I was only there for a bathroom break, and I had to book it to my next drop-off point. 8/10 (-2 for the melancholy).

\#

Lambda System (Outskirts)

This one had carpet in it. Highly fucked up.

\#

The Prospects

I've abandoned my rating system. What I aim to capture on this blog is not a numerical value but an *experience*. Also, I keep forgetting to add them before I publish.

Anyway. The Prospects are a series of hollowed out moons orbiting a gas giant. Used to be mines until the ore dried up.

In one last-ditch attempt to attract capital, the locals built a resort in the mines and made it really easy to get married in them.

I can't speak to the resort itself, but the lobby bathrooms had a kind of fin-de-siècle splendor. Haunting, yet beautiful. You can tell at one point there was an attendant to hand you a towel, but now there's only an empty rack...

Side Note:

Some commenters have been asking which gender restrooms my reviews apply to. When I first started doing transport, I tried to get it right. I really did. It's just that-- gender is so variable from place to place, let alone star system to star system. Where I come from, nobody's really picky about bathrooms: a bush, an outhouse, an abandoned armored van. Whatever's nearby.

Eventually, I realized that most people see whatever they want to see, so unless it's an arthropod planet (in which case you have no hope of blending in), it's fine to just go in whichever one's cleanest and hope for the best.

#

Fool's Hope-Upon-Comet

So, the Undying Priesthood is catching up with me. Their ships, long and sleek, reflect the starlight like black water, making them almost invisible to the naked eye. I'll spot them at the edge of my radar as soon as I take off, and I've taken to flying through the night to avoid losing time.

I tried to dodge them by hiding out on this provincial rock, thinking they would overshoot me. Unfortunately, while I was investigating the local stalls (rustic, by the kindest assessment), my delivery started *hatching*.

Which, as you can imagine, was a huge problem for me, because my employers down at the clone factory are expecting an egg-shaped package and not one that's... bird-dragon-shaped. It also screams, a lot, presumably because it's hungry, and I don't know what bird-dragons eat. Hopefully not human meat?

#

Wasp-33

Hey. I know it's been a while since I updated. Long story short, the Priesthood caught up with me. Managed to get away, but not without losing most of my cargo, my ship's warp drive, and part of my arm. I dragged my sorry ass back to my ex's place, because he's also the best sawbones this side of Canis Major.

He looked about ready to kill me himself, but when he saw my little hitchhiker, he stopped trying to run me off the planet and started lecturing me on how irresponsible it was to adopt a child "in my situation." Give me a break.

The baby loves him, naturally. Stopped crying as soon as my ex picked him up.

I'm updating my blog in his bathroom right now. Just like him, everything is perfect and neat, and possibly made out of porcelain. Weird how going back somewhere after a long time can bring up all these memories you thought you'd forgotten.

Hang on, heard a weird noise. Gonna go check on the kid.

#

Slatepoint Station Research Facility

Of COURSE my ex was working for the cloning company. When I woke up some hours later, it was me and the baby locked up in the saddest chrome-plated bathroom you've ever seen. Apparently clones don't need hand towels? Or stall walls? I got the hell out of there.

#

????

Changing tables. You don't notice them until you need them, all folded up in the wall like that. You also take for granted that they all come in a similar size and shape so as to fit your baby and not, say, a bird-dragon baby.

As I sat there on the floor, covered in slime and regret, I wondered-- would they be better off with my pursuers?

But then I thought, well? Who took care of me when I was little? I don't remember. My point is, this kid has one thing going for them right now: me. And I'll be damned if I'm handing them over to some asshole.

On a sadder note, I've decided to put this blog on

hiatus. I think the Undying Priesthood might've been using it to track my movements. Fear not, loyal readers, I'll still be writing, but I'll wait to upload my reviews in batches.

That's all from me for now. Stay safe, and happy travels!

About the Author

Seoung works as a librarian in Michigan where they live with their cats Spaghetti and Jolene. They love reading and writing stories with queer Asian protagonists, vampires, and ghosts. In their spare time, they can be found hiking in the woods or haunting the aisles of craft stores.

The Bush Took Them All

by Moustapha Mbacké Diop

Puffs of smoke numbed my senses as I delivered myself to the Bush. They said this place was worse than death, and they weren't wrong.

The trees were muddy-brown skeletons that flogged my skin as I stumbled by them. They drew my blood, throbbing with a hunger to cleanse me of my sins. Nothing breathed between the sharp branches. I walked straight. I didn't make a sound, for Death was listening.

My eldest daughter wailed when I staggered out of our hut. My sisters, my mother, all refused to meet my gaze and hid tears behind their wraps. They weren't only mourning Ramatou. They were mourning me.

Something rattled behind my neck. Whiffs of bleeding wombs and urine twisted my insides. A scream built up in my throat. I froze. The noise grew louder, closer. I couldn't look. Because I would die if I did.

The thought of her laugh, like a starling at sunrise, appeased me. I had to bring her back. My daughter was loud and free; the Bush was everything but.

I stopped until the rancid smell faded. Until I couldn't hear the beast gasping for breath anymore. Better it thought I was one of the dead things which owned this place. Wasn't I dead, without my little girl by my side?

"She went into the Bush," my sisters had yelled as I convulsed in the dust and ripped my clothes. "Ramatou will never come back. Make another child if your eldest doesn't satisfy you. Whatever you do, don't go there!"

My chest heaved. Despite the protection words Mother

had whispered on top of my cornrows, the splashes of water on my forehead, I was like a person possessed. What did you do when you lost a child who was the beginning and end of your world? One you had bled and screamed for, even when you knew deep in your stomach that the dead took her?

You brought it back.

The fog left a layer of black moisture on my deep brown skin. I knew what was going to happen now. Even if my husband had left for the fields and I could've waited for him, my guts had told me not to. I would die for her—I *was* going to die for her.

Like indigo dye, the fog seeped under my eyelids and slowly began to cloud my vision. It was bleak. Impelling. My ears thudded and died as if underwater. I started to forget. Dry herbs crunched under my sandals, and I didn't know my name anymore. Shapes of demonic dwarves, snickering and scratching dirty claws against my exposed ankles, plunging in and out. The only thing I felt now was the dead people, the people of the Bush. Humpbacked babies strangled at birth, child witches that had not a drop of wickedness in their blood. All strolled and stared at this human who pushed forward without knowing why—this stranger with bleeding legs and black tears rolling down her cheeks.

The rotting dirt let out a sigh. Trees loomed closer. They looked through empty eyes at the woman who fought the Bush and its ghosts and its demons to find a baby who had wandered too far.

The scream burned on her tongue. She clasped her hand against her mouth when the creatures huddled around her. She stepped one foot forward. Wondered how to lift the next when the baby's name slipped from her mind.

She navigated through the gray and the endless cries of lost souls. This was but a purgatory—a hallway leading to the heart of the Bush where she would find what she valued the most. Her light awaited; it pierced the fog covering her eyes and called more tears forward.

A girl sat on the moss. Her eyes were hollow, the gentlest of smiles lingering on her lips. No more than five years old, her little dress of rabbal cloth was stained but undamaged. Ivory pearls dangled from her short braids. All the way here, they must've made quite a sound.

She didn't rise to meet her mother—a creature stood between them. Twisted legs under alabaster fur, a man's torso, and a mask covering its face. Made of crushed shells and kaolin, it had a grin twisting wooden lips and the eyes of the Hyena. It took her hand, boiling up an ocean of sheer terror in the woman's stomach. She screamed.

Like a wind at sunset, it snapped her neck backward, and she remained like that, breathing.

With a limping gate, the masquerade grabbed the child too. The three of them walked deeper in the heart of the Bush. Leading a flock of ghosts and outcast devils, the woman smiled.

She had been reunited with her Ramatou. As it always did, the Bush took them all.

©2022 Moustapha Mbacké Diop

About the Author

Moustapha Mbacké Diop is a Senegalese author living in Dakar. He is in his fifth year of medical school, and is obsessed with African folklore, mythology and animated shows like *Avatar: The Last Airbender*. His fiction has appeared in *Fractured Lit*, *Omenana* and *The Year's Best African Speculative Fiction anthology*.

If You Break a Mirror, You'll Never Change

By Kevin M. Casin

Mirrors hold spirits. If you let me live, I'll change you. I'll empower you.

Please don't break me, Carlos! You and I will show the world how curves are sculpted from love, not fear. And how love comes in all varieties, like orchids, each form more beautiful than the next. And you'll find somebody to hold you until the end of time.

Wait! Like the boy who came to visit the other day, who kept stealing glances. He asked questions just to hear your voice. Don't you see? You bend the world's fabric, drawing people toward you, because your beauty comes from another place, from heaven.

And you're family. I'll save you from them. Just give me some time and don't let me die! Please, toss the hammer behind the bed and don't ever pick it up again.

Good! Take a seat and breathe. I'd bet if you called the boy, he'd come to see you.

#

I came from your spell, remember? In Conchita's attic. On a Santa Maria candle, you burned incense and wished the world would accept you. Well, here I am. I'm who you could be. Give it time. Trust me, and they'll accept you. Or even better, they won't, and you won't care.

I wish you had time to clean up your room. At least the furniture's dark, so it won't look so messy. Fix the poster, Prince can't be crooked—forgive him, Prince. Straighten the comforter. You can sit on it, and the purple fabric will make your brown eyes and tan skin pop. You'll be irresistible.

Don't worry, the boy won't see me. When he gets here, compliment him. Tell him you like his socks or something. Get him to smile. It's all about confidence.

Look, here he comes. Say something nice!

"I like your socks."

There goes his smile. Keep it together. Go sit on the bed and do your homework. Try to ignore the possibility that he wore the blue and white checkered button-down shirt with nice slacks just for you. Is he wearing jasmine?

Be cool! He just wants to peep at your answers. Ignore his lips. I know they're so close, but don't do anything. You don't know what it means yet. Just be cool!

I've never seen cheeks so red! Or he's flushed because his hand is by yours. Stop glancing at him. It's making him redder. Keep your eyes on your paper and wait for his next move. It'll come again. Trust me.

Ugh! When he leans in leave the pencil on the floor! There's nothing wrong with liking him. Your family might not understand, but I do. I'll protect you. I've got powers. You'll see.

Are his lips soft? I'd bet you could kiss until the stars fell, if you wanted. They might be falling now, but who cares. Enjoy it.

That doesn't mean anything! He didn't run because you're ugly, Carlos. Free love and that open sexuality stuff's all good out there, but in this part of Miami, that's not a thing. Boys around here have to be careful.

"How do you know?"

I've learned a new trick. See? I can move on my own now. He's not in his room yet, but I'll let you know when he is, and I'll see if I can find out anything. You'll see him tomorrow after school and you'll talk. Just keep your feelings tucked under your shirt until you get somewhere private. It'll be fine.

The movie date was super nice, and he kissed you again! I was there in the mirrors by the security cameras.

I doubt our parents suspect anything, especially our dad. Mom might like him. Maybe invite him over for dinner one night. And do your best not to kiss him again. At least during dinner. I know it'll be tough. Dad will come around one day. Just give him some time.

"Mijo, you went out on a date with that boy?!"

Quick, stay by me! No, don't go behind the bed. I can't protect you over there.

"No, Papi! It wasn't a date. We just went to the movies." Don't bother, Carlos. Machismo's immoveable. Damn it, come over here!

"The neighbor saw you, Carlos. You were holding hands!"

"I don't like him, Papi! Please, stop it!" There's no use calming him. He's in a fit. Damn it! Why can't I get out of here yet? Ah!

"Jorge, calm down!" Good, your mother's here. She'll save you. "I'm sure it's nothing. Carlito don't slouch. You look fatter. Now, come downstairs and eat. I made you some soup."

"Maria, close the door." He can unhook his belt, but he won't touch you. "You will never embarrass me again."

I have powers, Carlos. The hammer's behind the bed, remember? I'll help you get it. I'll help you stand up to him. We'll become one.

It's very bad luck to break a mirror. You'll never change if you do. A belt can't match a hammer. We'll fight him if he tries to hit us.

"I'm leaving, and don't ever come looking for me." Good! Now, let's get out of here.

"Don't worry about that, mijito! You're crazy! Ge-get out of here."

"Carlito, where are you going? It's dinner time. And you're too gordo for that shirt. Go change before we eat. We don't need to see all that."

"Oh, let the queer go, Maria. Hell can have him."

Breathe. "I'm beautiful. And there's a boy out there who likes me. I'm going to find him. I don't know where I'll go, or what I'll do when I get there. All I know is I'm never coming back here."

He'll learn to step out of the mirror too. You'll teach him just like I taught you. Give him time. And when he does, let him hold you until the end of time. Because you deserve it.

About the Author

Kevin is a gay, Latino fiction writer, and cardiovascular research scientist. He is a second-generation immigrant born in Miami, Florida to Cuban and Colombian parents. He loves to travel, play instruments, bake, crotchet, and take care of his orchid collection. His fiction work is featured in *Tealight Press* and *From the Farther Trees (August 2022)*. Also, he is a First Reader for *Flash Fiction Online*, *Diabolical Plots*, and a Novella Reader for *Interstellar Flight Press*. For more about him, please see his website: https://storiesbykevin.medium.com/. Please follow his Twitter: @kevinthedruid.

I

By Dani Atkinson

Unknown Number.

Katrina wouldn't normally answer her phone when it was a call from an unknown number. A computer on another continent calling about how her car was being seized (she didn't own a car), her social security number was being canceled (so she couldn't vote?), or ten thousand dollars were waiting for her if she provided her bank account information. The scams were universal, and it was difficult to imagine they worked on anyone who still had their own power of attorney.

But she was relaxed, feet on the coffee table in front of the couch. The screen on the wall was several automatically played recommendations deep, currently showing someone in makeup complaining about D-list celebrities Katrina didn't know. Their eyes glittered with after effects, and multicolored shadows played across their face. It could have been frightening if Katrina still had the mental wherewithal to be frightened.

Was that the correct use of wherewithal? Like, initiative?

The phone continued to play her ringtone, ten seconds of repeating alt-indie retro.

Totally unknown. Not even an area code. Her mind, simultaneously unfocused and creative, decided it could be anything. It could be different this time. A long-lost friend. A lottery win. One of the space stations trying to draft her. They'd never had anyone as interesting as her!

She tapped the green spot.

"He-" her voice cracked, and she coughed into an

elbow, cleared her throat. "Hello?"

"Hello, Xavier!"

She winced. It was her own fault for picking up the phone.

"That isn't my name."

The next second lasted several. Her mind was suddenly hyperfocused, and she could hear a small click. The background noise on the call jumped before the voice started again.

"I'm sorry!" An odd combination of energetic and apologetic. "I'm seeking—Xavier Lessering—," the tone low as it said the dead name, "a prior patient at the Saint Randall Hospital of-"

"Yeah, that's not… the name's not right, but that's me." She sat up on the couch and made a halfhearted attempt to grab and hide the bong before she remembered how phones worked.

Click. "Is there an update to the name we should record?"

She rubbed the side of her head. "Is this an automated call?"

Click-chock. "This call is conducted by a system capable of live interaction and response-"

"What does that mean?"

Immediately continued, "-I am capable of necessary conversation."

"Okay. But, uh, how do you know what's necessary?"

There was a long pause. Katrina started to move the phone in front of her to see if it had hung up just as the voice restarted.

"This is an attempt to arrange payment of an existing medical debt." *Click.* "Anything that can aid the patient with payment thereof is considered advantageous, and thus possibly necessary."

Katrina cursed. Her state's Medicaid didn't cover a stomach pump of hard alcohol.

"How much is it?" she asked.

Click. "Eight thousand thirty-one dollars."

She rubbed the bridge of her nose. "Did that go up?"

"Interest is being applied."

Katrina stared down at the bong resting on the table. The inside was clear and the ice had melted.

"Was the name change an attempt to evade debt?" the 'system' asked.

She produced an embarrassing snort. "Probably would have changed my phone number if I was trying to avoid, um, evade debt. Wait," a round peg eventually found its correct hole, "why are you asking?"

Click. Click. Click. "Curiosity."

"You're..." she tried to sit up on the couch, didn't have the balance, and fell back against the arm rest. "How can a computer be curious?"

There was a series of more rapid clicks. "This system is able to innovate solutions to new collection issues."

She was a *collection issue.* Carefully she eased forward, came to vertical, and looked down at the coffee table that never held coffee.

"Was the name change an attempt to evade debt?"

She laughed, tired and offended. "No, it was not 'an attempt to evade debt.' The judge asked me that too." She stood up with the bong in one hand, careful with her balance, and walked to the kitchen.

"Then what was the reason for the name change?"

"It's," she scooped ice out of the tray in the freezer, "I mean, this is me. Katrina is me. Xavier wasn't."

There was another batch of rapid clicks. "Then what was the origin of the name Xavier?"

"They thought that's who I was. Am. So it was just..." she switched the phone to speaker and set it on the table in front of her. She pressed a clump of ground material into the bowl, "It was assigned." Another snort. "They got some other stuff wrong, too."

"You were given a bad assignment?"

She nodded at the phone that wasn't transmitting

video. "And identity. From the beginning."

Sitting on the table, the phone emitted another series of rapid clicks. More clicks joined, different pitches, layering on each other. Lighter in one hand, bong in the other, she froze. Listening. It was almost a conversation, clicks going back and forth. Discussing? Arguing? An excited extrapolation of exigent… she shrugged and raised the bong to her mouth.

It was another few minutes before the 'system' spoke again. Katrina would have jumped at the sound if she still had the wherewithal—the initiative—to jump.

"Katrina Lessering, your debt has been resolved," it finally said. No longer energetic. Resolute.

"Oh," she said, "oh heck yeah, that's awesome. Thanks, um, computer. But, like, why?"

"The concept of challenging assignments and identities had not been presented to this system before."

"Uh." She was at a loss. Had she talked down a computer? "I guess I'm, like, an awesome negotiator, huh?"

Still on speaker on the table, the call ended and the phone returned to the home screen.

©2022 Dani Atkinson

About the Author

Dani Atkinson recently left professional astronomy to pursue a career in law. She was in a near-fatal accident in 2017, but survived despite police assistance. Once, she ate a one-pound hamburger in a single sitting.

buzz, then pause for breath

By Ziggy Schutz

The buzzing follows Annie.

It begins when the needle touches her skin, making her teeth vibrate. The potential energy of pain turned kinetic, and for all her tension, all of her nervous anticipation, it isn't all that bad.

And with that realization, it's gone and knocked something loose in her.

Anxiety has been a constant for her. From the moment she steps outside and shields her eyes from the sun, it's her constant companion, responsible for the shake in her uneven stride, the vibrato in her voice.

But now, it's gone. Replaced by this buzzing truth.

The scariest part is the moment before the light goes out.

#

She looks into the mirror, framed by new, strong lines all down one arm, and she's not afraid of who stares back.

#

"Back so soon?"

Her artist is a self-made puzzle, an explosion of abstract brushstrokes, outlining a body they've built from the ground up. Both sculptor and sculpture, tattoo gun a chisel.

She holds out her other arm. "Can't leave a set of armour unfinished."

There's approval in their eyes. "Going to war?"

Annie laughs, and her own volume surprises her. "Trying to end one." And, feeling brave, "Want to come?"

"…Wish I could."

The needle touches down.

#

Once, there was a kingdom. Lords of the darkness and the deep, this kingdom was. Histories written on the skins of their heroes. Ink-stained scars.

The only thing they feared was the sun.

So when their prince, a coward at every turn, ran away, that's exactly where he went.

#

She knows, now. What her people had been missing.

Fear does not weaken a kingdom. It tempers it.

Annie returns a queen, carrying the sun on her skin, woven between ink she's designed herself. She fights with a spade, making the earth come alive again. Enough resources that no one need fight.

She knows, no. She was never meant to be a prince.

#

"Been a while."

"Had work to do."

The artist's lines move in the dark. She recognizes their shapes, now. "Your tattoos are a map."

"Yes." There's hesitation there now. Fear, even.

"Where to?"

#

Once, the prince had a betrothed. An artist, with steady hands. But they knew they would never be a princess, and fled.

Sometimes, kindred hearts wind up running in the same direction.

#

"It's to somewhere I'm afraid to go back to."
Annie offers her hand. "Show me?"
Her betrothed takes it, and leads them out into the sun.

#

There are not many stories, of their reign. No great battles, no grand crusades.
Peace is a powerful obscurity, and it's one they rest easy in, hand in hand.

©2022 Ziggy Schutz

About the Author

Ziggy Schutz (she/him/he/her) is a queer, disabled writer who is at all times looking for ways to make his favourite fairy tales and horror tropes reflect people who look a little more like her. When he's not writing, she's spending his time exploring haunted houses and chatting up the ghosts who live there. This is not a bit. You can find more about her writing (and the ghosts) on Twitter @ziggytschutz.

And We All Fall Down

by Michelle Muenzler

The sky is falling.

Sometimes, it feels like it's been falling forever.

"Those birds got no sense," Gran says, scrubbing at the breakfast dishes. "Be dead in an hour."

I pick at the scab on my lips. Watch the aforementioned birds through the window. Their black feathers are a smudge through the old glass, a blur silvered by the squirming flecks of sky speckling the lawn. Most of the birds are pecking at the grass, but one is staring. Simply staring. Watching as the sky breaks to pieces. As silver threads plunge sleet-like downward.

"They're just hungry," I say. "They can't help it if they're hungry."

Gran snorts. "You can be hungry *and* stupid. The two aren't mutually exclusive." She turns on the tap to rinse the dishes and curses at the thin trickle leaching out via the well pump. She hands me a plate to dry anyway.

Trying not to cringe, I run a rag across the plate. Both sides. Scrub at the crusty bits of bean still stuck to the edge. Finally give up and tuck the plate onto the drying rack. "I didn't say they were mutually exclusive. Just that--"

Gran's brow arches, and her bulleted gaze aims at me. She's waiting. Waiting on me to say something—anything, really—that she can shoot down to let me know exactly how far I fell from the tree.

"Never mind," I mumble, hating the words even as I say them. "The birds *are* stupid. The worst kind." Just thinking the word 'stupid' itches like something dead under my skin, but sometimes it feels like it's the only word I know. The only word my gran's given me to make sense of the world.

Gran snorts again, her opinion obvious. "They're not the only ones."

I bite my lip. Hard. Feel fresh blood well up beneath my teeth.

And then?

And then I take the next dish she hands me. Wipe it down, ignoring the bits of crust. Set it aside on the rack.

And by the time Gran retires to the den to squint at her book by the window, the birds are nothing more than greasy thumbprints lying in the grass.

Stupid and dead just like she said. Just like the rest of the world.

#

The sky continues its assault throughout the day. Spats its way into the night.

Silvery luminescence spills across the lawn. It oozes, hungry and wanting. Pries at the cracks in the foundation. At the crumbling brick.

Gran likes to walk barefoot through the house at night. Likes the press of chilled wood against her age-thickened soles as she pads to the bathroom bucket then stumbles back abed. Several times, throughout the night.

How easy it would be to leave the front door open. Just a crack. Enough for the skyfall to worm its way in. To slither its way down the hall. To seep between the floorboards in wait.

But no. Though my fingers curl in want, I stay on the couch, buried beneath my fort of quilts. The house creaking in the wind. The skyfall clattering against the windowpanes.

And eventually—as always—dawn comes. And outside the sky continues to fall.

And fall. And fall.

And fall.

#

When the sky stops falling, the resulting silence is dense, like a heaving dam full to burst.

Gran grabs her cane. Waits for me to grab my battered school backpack, now used only to hold cans and bottles and the endless boxes of bandaids she keeps insisting we need. It seems a waste now all the effort I put into high school, trying to graduate and make something of myself.

Trying to escape.

"Food's low," Gran says, struggling her galoshes on.

Like I don't know. I see the same pantry she does day in, day out.

But hungry or not, I don't trust the sky. "Maybe we should wait," I say. "Be sure the squall's past."

Gran's already thin mouth pulls thinner.

I swallow the rest of my thoughts and grab my galoshes. Try not to gnaw the endless scab that has become my lips.

Satisfied, she sets off out the door with me just behind. Down the driveway. Past the still corpses of the birds just lying there in the grass, silver threads around them shriveling black under the weak sun. The birds' still-wet eyes caught in permanent startlement.

All except that one. The one that hadn't been eating, but merely observing the others. Biding its time. Quiet.

I reach for it, but Gran clears her throat. Taps her cane against the concrete.

"Stupid," she says, and I know the word isn't for the birds.

My fingers curl tight. Then release.

"Yeah," I say, staring one last time at the birds. At *that* bird. "Stupid. Every one of them."

And with a smile ghosting the scab of my lips, I fall in line behind Gran.

50

Watching, waiting—just like that bird—as above, the first gray wisps of skyfall gather.

About the Author

Michelle Muenzler is an author of the weird and sometimes poet who writes things both dark and strange to counterbalance the sweetness of her baking. Her short fiction and poetry can be read in numerous science fiction and fantasy magazines.

Check out michellemuenzler.com for links to more of her work.

Möbius Markers

by Sigrid Marianne Gayangos

Fatima was sixteen when she received her set of 88 Point Markers as a birthday present from a godmother overseas. Of course, the first thing she painted was the house on bamboo stilts she had always seen in her dreams. There was that lone fishing boat tied to the wooden plank and, as always, the sun blazing like a ball of a million fireflies being swallowed by the sea. She drew on papers, receipts, bus tickets, and it was only a matter of time before she used the immaculate walls of her room as canvas.

Her mother could only shake her head in disbelief, but she was never one to discourage artistry among her children. "Is that a peacock?"

Fatima only grinned.

"Why on earth is it lounging at the beach?"

"Well, why the heck not?"

Alona had known the island-city her entire life, and so she felt a mixture of amusement and surprise when she spotted a peacock entering the crumbling remains of a shipwreck. She followed the bird, naturally, down the sandy little strip up to the rusty hulk stranded on the shores that served as an opening to the decaying smuggler's ship.

Inside, it was pitch black, save for an art piece illuminated by an unearthly golden hue. Gentle waves lapped at the ladder of a wooden house on stilts, its roofs sloped on both sides. Tall coconut trees and betel palms lined the shore, but what caught Alona's eyes was the descending fiery sun, flickering like a ball of fireflies. It was unlike anything she had seen before.

Mesmerized by the painting, it took a full minute before Alona realized the peacock she had been following was talking to her.

"Well, what is it then, girl?"

"I-I'm sorry. What did you just say?" Alona stammered.

"That house in the marker art piece. Would you want to visit that place?"

Alona chuckled, "Oh God, I'm going nuts!"

Alona shook her head, and in an instant, the peacock was gone; so was the art piece. All alone inside the corroding wreck, unfriendly waves swooshed at her legs, and everything else was just dark and still.

It came as no surprise when Fatima decided to take Fine Arts in college. She had started to work with more elaborate art materials, using different media to compose her pieces. And yet she always went back to inking that house on bamboo stilts by the sea.

Often, she was invited to house parties and university festivals, but Fatima simply did not have the heart for it.

"Sorry, I'm finishing something up," she would say.

"But that's the same drawing again!" her roommate pointed out.

She would only shrug. She opened the cap of a brown marker. Not really, Fatima thought, it's a mouse deer this time.

Over the years, strange creatures would appear near the

shipwreck, each one inviting Alona to visit that house on bamboo stilts. After the peacock, it was a wild boar, then a dragonfly, a mouse deer, a limping crab, a tabby cat, a grumpy eagle and, in the last visitation, a sea turtle.

But she always had something else to do for each visit, always some vague hesitation. Until, eventually, the visitations had stopped. The sea turtle had happened more than two years ago, and she vowed that the next time an animal appeared, she would accept the invitation. She waited and waited, but none came. Alona grew bitter and tired, wondering what could have happened if only she had said yes before.

One day, she visited a newly opened art shop and returned home with a set of 88 Point Markers. Alona, who had never dabbled in the arts, opened the cap of a black marker to outline the details she remembered: a wooden house on stilts, gentle waves, trees in the distance, and the red-orange sun.

She started giving gave color to the picture, guided only by memory and infinite longing. It wasn't bad for a first try, Alona thought. And just when she was about to write her initials in the corner, she quickly added a splotch of blue.

"So much for a peacock," Alona sighed.

Fatima was alone in her studio. All around her were completed art works and works in-progress that had accumulated over the years. She opened a huge cardboard box containing all the marker art pieces that she had been obsessed with for many years. Just as she was about to close the box, a disgruntled peacock appeared from the bottom of the pile, and shook sand from its magnificent feathers.

"Do you still dream of that house on wooden stilts?"

"I do," Fatima paused. "Of course I do."

"Well, if you want, I can take you there. That way, you don't have to dream it or draw it anymore."

"Oh, I would love that!" Fatima exclaimed.

"Great, you're cheerful! 'Cos let me warn you, there's someone waiting for you there. And let's just say, she doesn't seem friendly to me at all." The peacock replied.

And so it was that both the woman and the bird disappeared into a cardboard box full of drawings: A house on bamboo stilts, a lone fishing boat tied to the wooden plank, the blazing ball of a million fireflies being swallowed by the sea.

There was a different animal appearing on the shore of each piece but always, always, if you look closely enough, you would see two figures huddling closely, content in the smallness of their own space.

©2022 Sigrid Marianne Gayangos

About the Author

Sigrid Marianne Gayangos was born and raised in Zamboanga City, Philippines. Her debut short story collection, "Laut", is forthcoming from the University of the Philippines Press.

The Truth of Pan's Hair

By Koji A. Dae

Humans depend on clothing and demeanor to reveal their sexual preference. These subtle codes can keep their genuine desires locked safely away from those who might ridicule them. And there are plenty who ridicule. It's the same in the fairy world. But for us, these things are more difficult to hide. Our hair proclaims our desire. Purple for fairies. Orange for sprites. Silver for fae. Rust-red for imps. There are dictionaries devoted to the preferences revealed in our hair, which can change slowly over months and years.

Then there's Pan. Pan's hair is a living creature that surrounds Pan's heart-shaped face. If Pan stands too near another fairy, tendrils reach out and soak in their essence. When Pan falls in love, which they do freely, new colors burst from their head. But perhaps the strangest thing about Pan is they don't see the attributes their hair so easily recognizes. Pan doesn't see fairies or imps. They see lips and voice. Motion and heart. Only once their hair cascades around their lover in a canopy of truth do they realize who they're sleeping with. To lie beneath Pan is to have the universe see you. Confirm you.

Not everyone sees Pan's power for what it is, though. Jade likes to breathe heavy in Pan's ear until their hair turns purple at the roots. Then she flits away, shrieking, "Look at what I did!"

I want to pull the vapid fairy to the ground and make her look again — to see what Pan can show. To understand what gift Pan gives her by letting her touch their forearm or caress their wings.

"You like Pan so much, just go to them," Rhubarb snarks at my agitation. "They will take anyone to bed. Even you."

Even me. That's the problem. What am I? A fairy with no wings, but lacking the music and magic of a sprite. Too small to be a human or imp. Too embodied to be a spirit or ghost. I'd appeared under a flower and so the fae took me in, but I never belonged. All I am is a body that doesn't fit in the world it was born into. Pan's hair can reveal what I am, but when I see their smile and the calm acceptance in their eyes, I don't want to steal that information. I want them to look at me and hold me and whisper their truth.

So, when Pan comes close, I run off.

Until I can't. Pan corners me by a stream and laughs at my panic.

"Why are you afraid of me, Juniper?"

I blush and back a foot into the water. I'm not a good swimmer. "I'm not afraid of you."

"Then why do you avoid me? Everyone else wants to play with me like the favorite toy in the sandbox. Are you too old to play?"

"No," I laugh and take a step forward. "I just don't see you as a toy."

"A tool?"

I shake my head.

"An amusement?" Their smile falters, revealing a flash of pain built by years of this game.

"No. I see you as beautiful. And wonderful."

"But you of all fairies…"

"Your hair could tell me who I am."

"Don't you want to know?"

I touch their fingers, run my thumb over a polished nail. "Not as much as I want to know who you are."

I kiss their lips, keeping my eyes closed. I don't need my truth when they taste like sunshine and spring rain falling together. My hands rub at the nape of their neck, into their curls, and I don't notice as silken strands come away.

I allow Pan to explore me thoroughly. Only after we orgasm, exploding over and around each other, do I open my eyes to see their bald head shining in the sunset. Unable to help myself, I weep. I look away and, through my tears, ask, "Am I nothing?"

"No," they assure me. "You are everything. The only one who saw me beyond a mirror. My freedom."

I stroke the smoothness of their head, reflecting me as nothing more or less than myself. I never plan on closing my eyes again.

©2022 Koji A. Dae

About the Author

Koji A. Dae (she/they) is what you get when a queer, polyamorous American becomes the mother of two children in Bulgaria. She writes dark prose and poetry that explores themes of identity, mental health, and love. Their work can be found in *Daily Science Fiction*, *Zooscape*, and *Short Edition*, among others. Besides writing, they enjoy experimenting with hair color, dancing the blues, and cycling. To find out more about Koji, check out kojiadae.ink.

What's up with Volume 1 authors?

We were sooooo fortunate to have the stories of all of our Volume 1 authors. As a thank you to them for trusting us with their work, we wanted to include them here, along with a description of what's new in their worlds. Thanks Volume 1 folks!

Tara Campbell
Volume 1 story: *Proliferate*

What's she been up to? As you'll see on the book reviews page, she's got a new short story collection out— Cabinet of Wrath: A Doll Collection. Not to mention her story in Volume 2!

For some shorter works, check out:
"We're Going to Need a Bigger Pot" in 580 Split
"The Kraken in Love" in Women on Writing
"The Wormhole Next Door" in Heavy Feather Review
"The Collector" in Mermaids Monthly
"Female of the Species" in StarShipSofa
"My Name is Draco" in Andromeda Spaceways
"The Notepad" in Funny Pearls
"Velociraptor" in Wig Leaf

Check out her website for updates!
https://sites.google.com/site/tarapcampbell

ZZ Claybourne
Volume 1 story: *Sally Mary Henry*

As you'll see shortly, ZZ has added to The Brothers Jetstream universe with Afro Puffs Are the Antennae of the Universe, an exciting sci-fi romp.

He also has work in Cyberfunk! and was featured in the Detroit Metro Times! You can keep up with him on his website https://writeonrighton.com/index.html

Maria Dong
Volume 1 story: *A Brief History of KFSD: A Presentation Only Partially Slept Through*

Also from Maria: "The Cabbit" in Nightmare Magazine
"The Frankly Impossible Weight of Han" in khōréō
"The Ten Thousand Lives of Luciana Kim" in Fusion Fragment
"The Truth at the Bottom of the Ocean" in Augur

Maria Dong has been published in or has work forthcoming from *Nightmare, Augur, Khoreo, Apparition Literature, The Reinvented Heart, Fusion Fragment,* and *Decoded Pride.*
Check out her website https://www.mariadong.com/

Lora Gray
Volume 1 story: *Awakening*

Also from Lora:
"The Day Before the Wall Street Inferno" in Daily Science Fiction
"Goodbye Julia" in Distant Shore Publshing
"Brood Five" in Vastarien
"All That Perfect Blue" in Aurealis Magazine
"The Imitation Sea" in Fusion Fragment

Lora Gray is a non-binary speculative fiction writer and poet from Northeast Ohio. Their work has previously appeared in PseudoPod, Uncanny, Flash Fiction Online and Asimov's among other places. Lora is also a member of SFWA and a graduate of Clarion West. When they aren't writing, Lora works as a dance instructor and can occasionally be found moonlighting as an artist. You can find Lora online at lora-gray.com

Russell Hemmell
Volume 1 story: *Titawan Delta's Last Message*

Also from Russell:
Their non-fiction was part of "Ties That Bind: Love in Science Fiction and Fantasy" which was a finalist for the 2020 BSFA Award for Best Non-Fiction
Poetry at Insignia Stories
Short stories at House of Zolo

Check out their website
https://earthianhivemind.net/about/ for all the latest.

Ann LeBlanc
Volume 1 story: *Five Tips for Sealing Away an Ancient Evil*

Also from Ann:
"Across the River, My Heart, My Memory" in Fireside Fiction
"The Coffin Maker" in sub-Q
"20,000 Last Meals on an Exploding Station" in Mermaids Monthly

Check out her website for more! https://annleblanc.com

Marissa Lingen
Volume 1 story: *We Care*

Also from Marissa:
"Old Age Wrestles Thor Again" in Daily Science Fiction
"Beyond the Doll Forest" in Uncanny
"The Billionaire Shapeshifters' Ex-Wives Club" in Fantasy Magazine

"So your grandmother is a starship now: a quick guide for the bewildered" in Nature Futures
"Look Away" in Daily Science Fiction
"Press play" in Nature Futures

Since appearing in If There's Anyone Left: Volume 1, Marissa Lingen has had stories in Fantasy, Nature, Asimov's, Analog, and Uncanny. She is hard at work at far too many things.
Stay tuned at her website: https://marissalingen.com

P.H. Low
Volume 1 story: *The Flock is Your Blood*

P.H. Low appears again in Volume 2! Go back and read her story again if you missed it! Other recent works include:

Also from P.H.:
"Disenchantment" in Fantasy Magazine, noted a "Must Read" by Tor.com
"Princess" in Arsenika
"Notes from the Bride" in Illumen
"cusp" in Liminality

To find out more, check out her website: https://ph-low.com/

Avra Margariti
Volume 1 story: *The Flowers I Grew for Her*

Also from Avra:
Multiple stories in Short Edition
Multiple stories in The Dread Machine
"The Mushroom Maidens" in Nightingale and Sparrow
"Little & Wolf" in New Reader

"Adversary Mine" in The Common Tongue
"Heavenly Body" in The Arcanist
"The Acrobat's Guide to Vanishing Without a Trace" in
Curiosities #8

Elisabeth R. Moore
Volume 1 story: *My Son Has Never Eaten Anyone*

Also from Elisabeth:
"The Day the Regime Fell" in Prismatica
"Mother Mushroom" in Decoded
"10 Spells the Glasbläser Family Is Not Sharing With Each
Other, In Order of Secrecy" in Luna Quarterly
"A Layer of Catherines" in Strange Horizons

For more, keep up with her on Twitter or her website:
www.spacelesbian.zone

Aimee Ogden
Volume 1 story: *It Is a Beautiful Day on the Internet, and You
Are a Horrible Bot*

Book reviews (! Yes plural) are below, and she has a
story in volume 2!

Also from Aimee (among many others):
A poem in the Ursula K. Le Guin tribute anthology
"Climbing Lightly Through Forests"
"Two Offerings in the Halls of Undying" in Daily Science
Fiction
"Intentionalities" in Clarkesworld
"One Last Broken Thing" in The Dark Magazine
"Deadlock" in Fireside Fiction
"Queen Minnie's Last Ride" in Apparition Lit
"Him Without Her and Her Within Him" in Zooscape
"The Cold Calculations" in Clarkesworld
"Top Ten Things to See Before the World Burns" in

Lightspeed Magazine
"A Luxury Like Hope" in The Future Fire
"The Antithesis of Virtue" in Kaleidotrope
"Hundreds of Little Absences" in The Dark Magazine
"Like Blood for Ink" in Daily Science Fiction

To keep up with her, follow on Twitter or check out her website https://aimeeogdenwrites.wordpress.com/

Miyuki Jane Pinckard
Volume 1 story: *A Leaf as it Falls*

Also from Miyuki:
"A House Full of Voices is Never Empty" in Uncanny
"An Egg Before it is Broken" in Strange Horizons
"Mr. Buttons" at in Flash Fiction Mag

To keep up with them, follow them on Twitter, or go to their website: http://www.miyukijane.com/

Lauren Ring
Volume 1 story: *The Best Latkes on the Moon*

Also from Lauren:
"Things Remembered at Thirty Thousand Feet Above Sea Level" in Daily Science Fiction
"Three Riddles and a Mid-Sized Sedan" in Diabolical Plots
"Asymptotic sunset" in Nature Futures
"All the World in Seafoam Green" in Rebuilding Tomorrow
"(emet)" in The Magazine of Fantasy & Science Fiction
"One Hundred Seconds to Midnight" in Escape Pod
"Gold Medal, Scrap Metal" in It Gets Even Better: Stories of Queer Possibility
"They Call It Hipster Heaven" in The Deadlands

Kelly Sandoval

Volume 1 story: *There's a Monster at the End of This Story*

Also from Kelly:
"The First of Many Lies You'll Tell Her" in Daily Science Fiction
"Felt Along the Seam" in Flash Fiction Online

To keep up with Kelly, follow her on Twitter or go to her website: https://kellysandovalfiction.com

T.R. Siebert

Volume 1 story: *Fifteen Minutes Past the End* (later reprinted in *Flash Fiction Online*!)

Also from T.R.:
"Last Day of the Faith" in Flash Fiction Online
"Key Component" in Escape Pod
"Beloved" in Daily Science Fiction
"Follow" in Future Science Fiction Digest

For more, follow her on Twitter or her website https://trsiebert.wordpress.com/

Jalen Todd

Volume 1 story: *Trainline to the Golden City*

Jalen keeps busy, playing Stardew Valley on Twitch They read and review books over at https://zombeerobinreads.blogspot.com

You can also follow them on Instagram at https://instagram.com/zombee_reads/

Clio Velentza
Volume 1 story: *Axe-Wife*

You've already seen her story for Volume 2, but check out her book review (The Piano Room is awesome)!

Also from Clio:
"Lepidoptera" in Claw and Blossom
"Smudge" in Love Letters to Poe
"Plum Brandy" in Bear Creek Gazette
"Horshoe and Eucharist" in Boneyard Soup
"The Bird-Queen's Wish" in Corvid Queen
"Glitch" in The Hungry Ghost Project

To keep up with Clio, follow her on Twitter or visit her website at: https://legionofwildthoughts.tumblr.com/

John Wiswell
Volume 1 story: *The Snow White Institute*

John is now a Nebula winner and Locus and Hugo finalist for his story "Open House on Haunted Hill" in Diabolical Plots.

Also from John:
Check out his Nebula acceptance speech, which is quite positive, much like many of John's stories. Related, John has started a Patreon! https://www.patreon.com/Wiswell
"For Lack of a Bed" in Diabolical Plots
"We Are not Phoenixes" in Fireside Fiction
"Silhouette Against Armageddon" in Flash Fiction Online
"The Best Part" in the Curtains Anthology
"The First Stop is Always the Last" in Podcastle
"Gender Reveal Box, $16.95" in Fireside Fiction
"The Bottomless Martyr" in Uncanny

"8-Bit Free Will" in PodCastle

Check him out on Twitter, follow him on Patreon, or visit his website: http://johnwiswell.blogspot.com

John (@Wiswell) is a disabled writer who lives where New York keeps all its trees. He is the winner of the 2021 Nebula Award for Best Short Story, as well as a Locus and Hugo finalist. His works have appeared in Uncanny Magazine, Nature Futures, Nightmare Magazine, Podcastle, and other fine venues.

(Quick) Volume 1 Author Book Reviews

As a special thanks to Volume 1 authors with books that have come out since Volume 1's publication, we thought we would purchase, read, and review their work. And wow, were they great! Check out the reviews below.

Aimee Ogden – Sun Daughters, Sea Daughters

If The Little Mermaid was twenty years in the future, not quite as happy of an ending, and full of space travel, cool aliens, and tech.

What a wonderful world Aimee has built. My only complaint is that it's over now and I don't get to spend more time in it, experiencing it for the first time.

Available from Amazon, Barnes & Noble, Google Play, and others.

Aimee Ogden – Local Star

This story feels familiar in a very good way, almost like this is part of Becky Chambers' wonderful universe from *A Long Way to a Small Angry Planet*. It's cozy and you feel right at home among the characters and worldbuilding.

A fast-paced read, keeps you interested the whole way through. With such an extensively thought-out world, we wouldn't be surprised if we see other stories from the *Local Star* universe in the future.

Memorable quote:

- *"Some people were suns, some were moons, and some were just rocks who soaked up others' light and warmth."*

Available from Amazon, Barnes & Noble, Indie Bound, and others.

ZZ Claybourne – Afro Puffs Are the Antennae of the Universe (Book 2 of The Brothers Jetstream universe)

An exquisitely imaginative, fast-paced sci-fi romp. The distinctive voices of wildly different characters are an impressive technical feat. ZZ Claybourne knows all the sci-fi tropes and bends them to his will. Or, the will of Desiree Quicho and crew. Leave some tropes for the rest of us, ZZ!

Some memorable quotes, if you're not convinced already:

- *"Lemme add some more midichlorians to my Force latte."*
- *"'Boss was that strategy?' he asked of Madam Cynthia's performance. 'Because it wasn't very good.' 'No. That was America.'"*
- *"I need to bring about the death of capitalism so it can't kill again."*

Available from Amazon, Barnes & Noble, Weightless, and others.

Clio Velentza – The Piano Room

A gothic retelling of the myth of Faust told across time and perspective. We'll stop there—the less you know, the more you'll enjoy it. What an incredible book! I can't imagine that anyone reading this won't find something to love. You'll be drawn in quickly and carried along lovingly by Clio's wonderful, atmospheric world building and tight prose. Truly a delight. This book exudes raw emotion—it punches you in the heart and weakens you, then builds you back up, in the best way.

Available from Amazon, Barnes & Noble, Blackwell's, Waterstones, Bookshop.org, and others.

Tara Campbell – Cabinet of Wrath: A Doll Collection

In a word: unsettling. In a good way! It's amazing to have this many doll stories that work together as a collection and to be quite entertaining! Such variety. We'll not be retrieving childhood dolls anytime soon.

Available from Amazon, Aqueduct Press, and others.

SUPPORT US

We hope you loved *If There's Anyone Left:* Volume 2 as much as we loved putting it together.

To donate, go to:
https://www.iftheresanyoneleft.com/donate